Happy Ever After

For the 'Granby' babies
S.W.

ORCHARD BOOKS
338 Euston Road, London NW1 3BH
Orchard Books Australia
Hachette Children's Books
Level 17/207 Kent Street, Sydney, NSW 2000
ISBN 1 84362 528 8 (hardback)
ISBN 1 84362 536 9 (paperback)
First published in Great Britain in 2006
First paperback publication in 2006
Text © Tony Bradman 2006
Illustrations © Sarah Warburton 2006
The rights of Tony Bradman to be identified as the author
and of Sarah Warburton to be identified as the illustrator of this
work have been asserted by them in accordance with the
Copyright, Designs and Patents Act, 1988.
A CIP catalogue record for this book is available
from the British Library.
1 3 5 7 9 10 8 6 4 2 (hardback)
1 3 5 7 9 10 8 6 4 2 (paperback)
Printed in Great Britain

Tony Bradman

Happy Ever After

RED RIDING HOOD
TAKES CHARGE

Illustrated by Sarah Warburton

ORCHARD BOOKS

Little Red Riding Hood headed down
the woodland path, a basket of cakes
in one hand and a bunch of flowers in
the other.

It would be her first visit to Granny's for a while, and she hoped everything was OK. After all, it wasn't long since their scary experience with the Big Bad Wolf.

If it hadn't been for that nice
woodcutter...well, Little Red Riding
Hood hated to think what might
have happened.

She felt guilty, too. Anyone else would
probably have realised what the Big Bad
Wolf was up to. But she hadn't, and
Granny had almost paid a terrible price
for her mistake.

Little Red Riding Hood sighed - and made a mental note to be a lot more observant in future.

"Who's that?" Granny called out when Little Red Riding Hood knocked on the cottage door. "You'll have to show me some ID!"

"It's all right, Granny," said Little Red
Riding Hood. "It's me!"

Granny was pleased to see her, and
gave her a big hug and kiss.

"So then, how are you?" said Granny.
"Everything OK at school?"

"I'm fine," said Little Red Riding
Hood. "But how are you?"

"Oh, I'm all right," said Granny.
"Although I have to admit I do
sometimes get a bit lonely out here."

"Lonely?" said Little Red Riding Hood, a cake halfway to her mouth.

"Did I say lonely?" laughed Granny. "Take no notice, sweetheart, I'm all right really. Umm, these cakes are delicious, aren't they?"

Later that afternoon, Little Red
Riding Hood trudged homewards,
feeling more guilty than ever.

She should have realised Granny was
lonely! It was obvious - Granny didn't
have any neighbours, and Mum and
Little Red Riding Hood lived too far
away to visit her regularly.

"Hello there, Little Red Riding Hood!"
a voice roared suddenly. A large, hairy
figure had appeared on the woodland
path beside her.

"Yikes!" she squeaked. "Oh hi, Mr
Woodcutter. Sorry, you startled me."

"No problem," boomed the woodcutter, smiling at her. He was a big man with a big beard, and around the same age as Granny. "Er...just been to see your Granny?" he said. "How is she?"

"OK, thanks," said Little Red Riding Hood. "Well, mostly OK..." She told him what Granny had said.

"A wonderful woman like your Granny feeling lonely?" he said. "I can hardly believe it! I would have thought she'd have plenty of visitors...

"Still, we are rather isolated in this part of the forest. I get a bit lonely myself sometimes. So maybe I could, er...pop over and see her?"

"Don't worry, Mr Woodcutter," said
Little Red Riding Hood. "It's kind of
you to offer, but I'm sure I can think of
something. Anyway, I'd better be getting
home now. Cheerio!"

That evening, Little Red Riding Hood sat in her room feeling bad. She would just have to visit Granny more often. Although that might not be easy - there was hardly a day when she didn't do something after school.

Anyway, the next day, she thought she could get to Granny's and still be back in time for swimming.

Granny was surprised, but pleased, of course. And she seemed even more pleased when Little Red Riding Hood passed on the woodcutter's regards.

"He asked after me?" said Granny, patting her hair. "Did he really?"

Little Red Riding Hood couldn't stay long. She hurried back, but she was late for swimming.

She went to see Granny the next day,
and the next, and the day after.

And she was late for her piano lesson, and karate...

...and she nearly missed Brownies altogether. Brown Owl was not happy.

There was another problem, too, Little
Red Riding Hood thought as she
trudged homewards one day. She was
fast running out of things to talk to
Granny about - at least, things that
Granny might find interesting.

"Cheer up, Little Red Riding Hood!"
somebody roared. She jumped, but she
knew it was only the woodcutter. "Why
the glum face?" he said, and Little Red
Riding Hood explained what was
worrying her now.

"I'm sure Granny loves seeing you, whatever you talk about," said the woodcutter. "Mind you, it can be a bit tricky with such a big age gap. Maybe your Granny could do with company of her own age from time to time, someone she's got more in common with, and I, well, I..."

"You might be right..." said Little Red
Riding Hood before he could finish
what he was going to say. "It's worth a
try, anyway! Cheerio!"

That evening, Little Red Riding Hood
searched The Forest Web, and soon
found something that looked promising.
She put Granny's name down for
it straightaway.

"The club is called The Forest Belles, Granny," she said on her next visit. "And it's for people just like you - old ladies who live on their own. They meet twice a week, they go on great outings - I bet you'll love it!"

But Granny didn't. She hated it, and
stopped going after a week.

"I'm sorry, sweetheart," she said, "but being with a bunch of old ladies isn't my cup of tea. I mean, all they did was gossip non-stop and moan."

Little Red Riding Hood trudged homewards down the woodland path, even more worried than ever, and bumped into the woodcutter again.

"Ah, I take it things aren't going well," he boomed.

Little Red Riding Hood explained about The Forest Belles.

"Can't say I blame Granny for feeling that way," said the woodcutter. "Sounds to me as if she'd prefer the company of one person, a chap, perhaps, and I could always, er..."

"I don't know, Mr Woodcutter," Little Red Riding Hood murmured gloomily. "It would have to be the right person, and who could that be?" The woodcutter beamed broadly at her, but she took no notice. "Umm, you do have a point, though," she said. "Thanks for the advice. Bye!"

The Woodcutter's shoulders sagged, and he sadly turned away.

That evening, Little Red Riding Hood surfed The Forest Web again, and she soon found something else that looked promising...

"It's called Forest Speed Dating, Granny," she said on her next visit, "and they have a Senior Citizens Night at the Palace Community Centre. You'll meet loads of nice people, maybe even somebody special."

But Granny didn't. She hated it even
more than The Forest Belles

"I'm sorry, sweetheart," she said, "but I'd rather spend a bit more time with someone, so we can get to know each other. It was all too quick."

That evening, Little Red Riding Hood trudged homewards through the darkening forest. She was filled with gloom. What else could she do?

She came round a bend in the path, and there was the woodcutter. He asked after Granny, and they chatted for a while. But then he sighed.

"Well, I'd better be off," he said. "Oh, I meant to tell you - I'm, er...thinking of moving away...to start a new life somewhere else."

"Really? How wonderful!" said Little Red Riding Hood. "Well I ought to be getting home myself. All the best, Mr Woodcutter. Bye!"

She carried on down the path, thinking about Granny... And suddenly the answer hit her. She had known the right person all along - the woodcutter! Why hadn't she seen it before? So much for being more observant!

She winced when she thought of how she'd put him off each time he'd offered to visit Granny.

And now he was planning to move away, and take Granny's chance of happiness with him. But Little Red Riding Hood decided she wasn't going to ruin things for Granny again...

So, the next day, there was a knock
on the woodcutter's door. He opened it,
and was rather surprised to see Little
Red Riding Hood there.

"Hi, Mr Woodcutter," she said. "I'm on my way to visit Granny, and I wondered if you'd like to come too. I'm sure she'd love to see you!"

The woodcutter smiled. "I thought you'd never ask," he said.

Granny and the woodcutter got on so well that within a month they announced they were getting married.

It was a wonderful wedding -
Little Red Riding Hood was
Granny's bridesmaid...

...and there was even a picture on the front page of *The Forest Times*.

And Granny and The Woodcutter and
Little Red Riding Hood (and even
Brown Owl!) lived...

HAPPILY EVER AFTER!

Written by Tony Bradman
Illustrated by Sarah Warburton

These books are available from all good bookshops, or can be ordered direct
from the publisher: Orchard Books, PO BOX 29, Douglas IM99 1BQ.
Credit card orders please telephone 01624 836000 or fax 01624 837033 or
visit our Internet site: www.wattspub.co.uk or
e-mail: bookshop@enterprise.net for details.

To order please quote title, author and ISBN and your full name and
address. Cheques and postal orders should be made payable to 'Bookpost
plc.' Postage and packing is FREE within the UK
(overseas customers should add £1.00 per book).

Prices and availability are subject to change.